Life in Cartoons!
The Complete Collection

Written & Illustrated by Steve Kang

Life in Cartoons! The Complete Collection

Written & Illustrated by Steve Kang

www.cat-astrophic.com

Copyright © 2019

First Edition

ISBN: 978-1-9991486-3-8

Contents:

Introduction:

"Life in Cartoons! The Complete Collection!" contains a total of 148 single panel cartoons. Categorized from childhood to adulthood, work to play, heaven and hell, relationships, and technology to the environment, it gives you a glimpse of why things are the way they are – some may not be as obvious.

What's it all about? Sadly true in many ways, viewing life from a low or susceptible moment in an animated media makes it less detrimental and even laughable. For example, having to go to the job you hate because of having to deal with that one idiot, or when the inner child in adults come out unexpectedly. We all have our bad days and the best way to look at it is with a grin.

Life in Cartoons began as part of the website *CAT-astrophic! The Astonishing Adventures of Sam & Roy!* It is a random collection of cartoons of everyday life with reoccurring appearances from Reggie and his cat, and topics like Office Chronicles, Lowbrow Thinking, and Stupid Stick People. All the cartoon panels have been scrupulously revised from its original version. This complete collection commemorates all cartoons made in the past decade or so, with a few that have never been seen or posted on the website. I hope everyone relishes the cartoons as much as I had fun making them!

Enjoy! ☺

Adulthood:

It's about not always being what you thought it would be.

"I know I'm watching cartoons. But
at least there's a moral at the end."

He refused to be labelled in that demographic because he has a full-time job and didn't live with his mother.

"I sneaked out of the office for this?!"

Never being objective, Reggie always
saw himself larger than actual size.

"I'm not sure why I watched the entire movie 'Gigli.' The part that sucks is I'll never get my two hours back."

"Yeah, that's nose hair in the sink. What else can it be?"

"Honestly... with things flopping around, do you really want to play volleyball on a nude beach?"

"Knock off the zombie act, Eugene! The coffee's ready!"

Botox gone wrong? Or right?

You know you're getting old when
Viagra commercials start looking good.

You know you're too old to be wearing miniskirts when construction workers look the other way.

"No, it's not the color of your shirt.
It's the way you have the collar up."

"I meant the other kind of mace for protection... the ones in a spray bottle."

"Why should I get life insurance?! It's not like I'm going to see a single penny of it!"

"I like to put my hand over the steering wheel because it makes me look cool."

19

Dating & Relationships:

It's about that girl you are in love with... which you
will never get.

The wine-in-a-box should have been a sure sign there would be no second date.

"When I said one of my fantasies were to date a superhero... I didn't mean with my own husband as one."

24

"So, this is how you're going to woo
her on Valentine's Day? If you ask
me, needs some serious work."

Stupidity is trying to impress your date
by dealing with the guy who cut line
when you know you'll end up in a coma.

Stockholm syndrome gone too far?

"These days it's the only way
to   get   Fred's   attention."

28

"Just because you're trying on a bra doesn't mean you understand feminism."

"I'm not sure why Mary the Mushroom doesn't like you. Everybody else thinks you're a fungi."

"How do I now she's a super-model? Well, for starters, she's not too bad on the eyes, chain smokes, and has a bottle of vodka."

"Who knows... maybe she's dating a clown because she has low self-esteem or needs a good laugh. Either way, the jokes on her."

"My wife's appetite grew after she quit smoking. She used to weigh 110 pounds. The tradeoff really sucks."

"Sure, I can remove the tattoo... but wouldn't it be easier to find another girlfriend with the same name?"

The feminist.

The masculinist.

Kids & Parenting:

It's about the achievements and disappointments of raising a child.

"Isn't Clyde so dreamy? The way he rides his tricycle into the sunset."

"You can never be too safe these days."

"Yes, Aileen! Junior is secure! I double checked!"

"Mikey is having problems with a fellow kindergartner, so he's watching reality shows to learn deception and intimidation."

"Look, ma! Another $999,919.75
more and I'll be a millionaire!"

"I never knew sports would bring so much joy and happiness to my life."

"You think I look weird? You should
check out the kid that made me."

"Son, can you teach me to shoot a gun?"

"Honestly, Elizabeth, what can I do? If I discipline him by spanking, it's child abuse."

"Yes, I know I've been watching cartoons and eating cereal all morning. It is what kids my age do on Saturdays."

"No way I'm having a bologna sandwich for lunch, mom! The standard sandwich for a second grader is peanut butter and jam!"

"Yupe! These added handlebar frills and flame decals increased my tricycle speed by 12 percent!"

Heaven & Hell:

It's about what heaven and hell is all about.

"What is the meaning of life? It is everything nice and nothing naughty."

"What is the meaning of life? It is everything naughty and nothing nice."

Lowbrow Thinking ©

"Sorry, Amy. We can't renege on our contract. The deal was at 27."

"Hey, Elvis! Read the sign!"

Office & Politics:

It's about that idiotic coworker or politician you want to kick in the behind.

"What do you mean by 'be more proactive?'"

The only reason Robert was invited
to board meetings was because
he did an awesome robot dance.

"You remember the good ol' days of sex, drugs, and rock n' roll? Now, it's about rap, crack, and drive by shootings."

"Salisbury steak, peas, mashed potatoes? What happened to the good ol' sandwich for lunch?"

"Sure, my boss is an annoying moron... but I don't think cutting her brake lines will resolve anything."

Office Chronicles ©

Lowbrow Thinking ©

Office Chronicles ©

A lawyer advises a lobbyist.

Lowbrow Thinking ©

Lowbrow Thinking ©

Politically incorrect.

Politically incorrect???

74

"What do I know about foreign policy?
Well, these here shoes are made in China,
which I bought at Walmart for $29.95."

"Hmm... I wonder if it's too late to change running mates?"

"What makes people think I have skeletons in my closet? I have no idea. Farrakhan, my head gear on right?"

The day after the election.

"Now I'm REALLY proud to
an American! WOO-HOO!"

Pets & Animals:

It's about the happiness and the nuances of owning a pet.

"This cat prefers new toys over crumpled paper and tinfoil... he's just not normal."

"I'm thinking of redecorating. Help me
move this castle an inch to the left."

Another mistake by Reggie was putting
the humane society on speed dial.

What your pets do when you are at work.

He knew he was double-crossed when
the chicken crossed the road again.

Reggie was shocked to learn he was being sued by his own cat for placing humiliating videos of him on the internet without his permission.

"Cat grass?! How barbaric!
Hasn't he heard of cilantro?"

89

"There's something just not right with a cat
smothered in suntan lotion... sunbathing."

"You see, here's the major difference between cats and dogs... there's no such thing as 'unconditional love' for us."

"Hey! Check it out! It's Ralph and the gang flying south... the hard way!"

The great standoff.

"He gets the munchies after
a bit too much of the catnip."

"Now, this kill took almost 20 minutes...
notice all the scratch marks on his face?"

"Rubbing your face into it will teach you to train your dog properly!"

"If you can get down from this tree anytime you want, how come you've been up here 8 hours?"

"What? Squirrels aren't allowed to spring clean?"

*"Cookies, doughnuts, cakes... are the humans trying to turn **us** into diabetics?"*

"Yeah, that's right... I called
you a bitch... a female dog."

101

Stupid Stick People:

It's about what stick figures are all about – all stick, no substance.

Stupid Stick People ©

Stupid Stick People ©

Stupid Stick People ©

Stupid Stick People ©

Stupid Stick People ©

The Oddballs:

It's about that oddball or odd thing that you think
and know is odd.

"I wear a red tie at the gym
because I'm the Govenator!"

"Hotdoggers. Sheesh!"

Reggie was very suspicious if the plumber was certified when he didn't see any butt crack.

"I swear, Aileen is wearing a wig."

Reggie always wondered why it took two cartoonists to make a comic strip... until he met them.

Reggie has an obsessive–compulsive disorder with cleaning. The upside of it was underneath the ceramic tiles was a hardwood floor.

Reggie thought the clown was using a whoopee cushion... but there was none to be seen.

"You want spare change? Why don't you
go work for it like that guy over there?!"

"Stuff on crime? Check out Dostoyevsky's Crime and Punishment... also the entire rap section in the music department."

"In my country, Speedo's still fashion yes."

Couch potatoes.

"AAARRG! The end is near!"

124

"Maybe we should tell him how things have changed in the past 40 years."

"No, I never in my life heard of
a doughnut store being robbed."

"Get well soon? You do realize
he has terminal cancer?"

127

"Well, at least he's not addicted
to any of that diet cola junk."

128

129

The lazy cartoonist.

"Patients with bad breath is one thing, but a dentist with bad breath is totally unacceptable!"

"Okay, men! Union rules strictly states one person works while others pretend to be busy!"

Technology:

It's about advancing human life and promoting our inner laziness.

"What do you mean how do I
know if this DVD is pirated?"

First, there was Beta versus VHS. Now, the gamble of this quarter century, HD DVD versus Blu-ray.

The day she knew what infamy meant was when she accidently sent her personal jpeg file to her entire email list.

"Just make sure there are enough flaws in Windows 7 so we can make tons of dough on the next 'new and improved' Windows operating system."

140

"Just as I thought... the bugs are starting to come out of Windows 7."

"I think I'll trash my cell phone."

142

Sometime next year...

"What is that, you ask? It's a Walkman.
Very popular in the eccentric eighties."

144

iPad conception.

A thousand years into human evolution and how technology made us fat, lazy, and stupid.

*"Texting while riding a motorbike?
Now that's seriously insane."*

The Future and the Environment:

It's all about doom – if we do diddly-squat.

"You want more ice in your drink? Don't you know there's a shortage of ice?"

"Hey, mack! You think gas is expensive? You know how much a gallon of water costs?"

"COUGH! COUGH! Darn secondhand smoke."

153

"Crap."

"I don't know, but lately I've been feeling nauseous and itchy. I think I have a bad infestation of humans."

"I don't get it... how are **we**
more of a pest than humans?"

"We can always dream."

In another part of the universe... far, far away...

"Damn you, BP! You killed my whale!"

"Eviction notice? What the..."

"Sure, the universe is vast. But to think there are other life forms is just ridiculous."

100,000 years ago on planet Earth.

A hundred thousand years into the future – human evolution due to too much texting.

"Acid rain? What acid rain? That's so eighties."

"You have chosen to see a thousand years into the future. Maybe you should have chosen the past."

"Global warming? No idea
what you're talking about."

The Holidays:

It's about if Santa will get you the gift you really, really want.

Reggie didn't fool anyone he was too old
for trick-or-treating... even in costume.

"Why do I want a million bucks for Christmas? Well, because of the current low interest rates and being a hot buyer's market for real estate... why not?"

"Hey, Martha! It's that strange kid again!"

"Okay... here's the deal..."

"It's that time of the year again to put
on our human disguises and be normal."

"Don't worry about your broken leg, Santa! The Flash will make sure all the toys will be delivered on time!"

175

"Wow, Wanda. You moved up to a Dyson vacuum cleaner from a broomstick. Nice!"

"Drat. A pink slip. I knew this would happen with China making all those toys at cut-rate pricing with no regard for safety."

177

Other great stories available in book and ebook format!

Includes the complete 481 CAT-astrophic! comic strips!
PLUS! The web version of Christmas Tale! & Halloween Night!

Written & Illustrated by Steve Kang

Written & Illustrated by Steve Kang

Written & Illustrated by Steve Kang

Written & Illustrated by
Steve Kang